Washoe Seasons of Life
A Native American Story

Karen Wallis
Diane Domiteaux
Illustrated by Lea Saling

Creative Minds Press

Reno, Nevada

Creative Minds Press
an imprint of **Beagle Bay Books**
Reno, Nevada
info@beaglebay.com

Book Design: Robin P. Simonds
Editing: Jacqueline Church Simonds

Visit our websites at:
http://www.creativemindspress.com
http://www.beaglebay.com

Library of Congress Control Number: 2004100855
ISBN: 0-9749610-3-5

First Edition
Printed in China
11 10 09 08 07 06 05 04   1 2 3 4 5

DEDICATIONS

I dedicate this book to my husband, Bob, my two sons, Chris and Eric, and my family and friends for their continuous love and support. I would also like to dedicate this book to colleagues, parents and students at Agnes Risley and Van Gorder Elementary Schools for being my inspiration.—*Diane Domiteaux*

This book is dedicated to Jim, my husband, two daughters, Tristen and Austin, my family and friends whose love and belief in me made it happen. It is also dedicated to the staff, parents and students at Mount Rose Elementary School who teach me something new and make me laugh every day.—*Karen Wallis*

I would like to dedicate my illustrations in this book to my family for their support during this endeavor. My parents, children and grandchildren have been a great source of strength. This has been an unforgettable and enjoyable experience.—*Lea Saling*

INTRODUCTION

Washoe Seasons of Life: A Native American Story is a historical fiction written to honor an ancient culture. The Washoe tribe, along with the Pauite and Shoshone tribes, carved their culture out of the harsh and beautiful environment we now call Nevada and California. The story is set in and around Lake Tahoe in the days before the coming of the white man.

Intended as a read-aloud book, *Washoe Seasons of Life: A Native American Story* is written in English. Throughout the book, you will find key nouns in bold italics. At the bottom of the page, those words are shown with their Washoe equivalent. For instance, the Washoe word for *any* lake is ***dá'aw***, but it is from this word that English derived the name ***Tahoe***. For the purpose of this book, we've used ***dá'aw*** to mean Lake Tahoe.

We are grateful to many members of the Washoe tribe who connected us with William H. Jacobsen, Jr., Professor Emeritus of Linguistics at University of Nevada, Reno, who has worked with the Washoe people since 1955. His efforts have ensured the preservation of this unique language, spoken by few in today's world. We thank him for his constructive critique of our usage and spelling of the Washoe language. A pronunciation guide, which he produced, can be found in the glossary.

Our hope is that *Washoe Seasons of Life: A Native American Story,* will be read for enjoyment, as well as for educational purposes, by all ages. This story is a snapshot into the past where survival was dependent upon seasonal fishing, gathering and hunting.

"Mele, come! Come quickly!" shouted her friend, Toso. "Hoya and Nuki are here!"

Mele hurried from the meadow of *the shore of Lake Tahoe* where she had been grinding dried fish and plants. The *grinding stone* clanged loudly when she dropped it on the *grinding surface* as she ran to Toso.

Toso and Mele had been impatiently waiting for their friends from the *Northern Washoe* to arrive at their summer camps at *Lake Tahoe*. Each year the families of Mele and Toso traveled to *the shore of Lake Tahoe* for the *summer*. It was Mele's favorite camp. She knew the fish, plants, berries and seeds would be plentiful. The lake was indeed the giver of life.

THE LANGUAGE OF THE WASHOE . . .

the shore of Lake Tahoe	**dá'aw 'á·ga'a**
grinding stone	**gámum**
stone grinding surface	**démge'**
Northern Washoe	**wélmelt̓i'**
Lake Tahoe / lake	**dá'aw**
summer	**čigá·bat**
Carson Valley Washoe	**p̓á·wa'lu'**
Washoe	**wa·šiw**
Southern Washoe	**háŋalelt̓i'**

Mele's and Toso's families were members of the *Carson Valley Washoe*, one of the three bands belonging to the *Washoe* tribe. Two summers ago, the children camped with the *Southern Washoe* who also belonged to the *Washoe* tribe. The *Washoe* fished and gathered plants, berries and seeds on the shores of beautiful *Lake Tahoe*.

The girls raced toward their friends. They were eager to see their *Northern Washoe* friends who camped with them last *summer*. Hoya and Nuki's father had cut his leg in a fall. His injured leg forced him and his family to stay at the *Carson Valley Washoe* camp while he healed. During their stay, the two families became friends as they fished and gathered plants together.

As Mele and Toso rushed toward Hoya and Nuki, they welcomed their friends with broad smiles. They excitedly pulled Hoya and Nuki back to their camp in the meadow. Mele ran to her mother. "*Mother*, may we play in the meadow?" Mele asked eagerly. She knew that she had not finished grinding the dried *fish* and *seeds* she had left on the *grinding stone*. She was not sure *her mother* would allow her to play before her work was finished.

Her mother hesitated as she glanced at the small pile of dried food. "Go play with your friends. You may finish the grinding later," she replied and smiled at the happy children.

THE LANGUAGE OF THE WASHOE . . .

my mother	**dilá'**
fish	**'áƚabi'**
seed	**ƚétik**
grinding stone	**gámum**
her mother	**dalá'**

The children raced to the meadow. Soon the shrieks and laughter of Nuki and the other *Washoe* boys rang throughout the meadow as they chased a buckskin *ball*. Mele, Toso and Hoya chattered like *magpies* as they traded stories.

THE LANGUAGE OF THE WASHOE . . .

Washoe	**waˀšiw**
ball	**ḱómol**
magpie	**ɫaˀɫat**

"*Children, children*, come! Time to eat!" shouted *Mele's mother*.

The hungry friends left their games and hurried to the *fire*. The delicious smell of roasting *fish* filled the air. After a blessing of thanksgiving, the two families shared their meal of *fish*, *wild onion* and *wild strawberries*. Mele, Toso, Hoya and Nuki quickly ate their *food*.

After eating, Mele remembered she had to finish grinding the fish and seeds. "*Mother*, thank you, thank you!" she shouted happily, when she realized the small pile of *food* was gone. Mother had finished her job so she could play.

Her mother smiled as she looked into the grateful eyes of her daughter.

THE LANGUAGE OF THE WASHOE . . .	
children	**ŋáwŋaŋ**
her mother	**dalá'**
fire	**dí'yu**
fish	**'áƚabi'**
wild onion	**bóšdi'**
wild strawberry	**ma'álaŋi'**
food	**démlu**
my mother	**dilá'**

Soon they all walked down the path to the sandy beach of ***the edge of the lake***. They found ***her grandfather*** and the other men of the tribe building the ***fire*** for the evening. Oh, how Mele loved to cozy up to the warm ***fire*** and listen to ***her grandfather*** spin her favorite stories.

THE LANGUAGE OF THE WASHOE . . .

the edge of the lake	**dá'aw 'á·ga'a**
her maternal grandfather	**de'élel**
fire	**dí'yu**

The happy chatter began to dwindle as they gazed into the glow of the *fire*. As the night sky's twinkling lights grew brighter, **her grandfather** slowly and softly began to chant. He opened his eyes and spread his hands up to the heavens and began to speak. Mele wondered if he would tell of **coyote** or **wolf**. But she could tell after his first few words that he was going to share her favorite *Washoe* legend about the weasel brothers.

The Language of The Washoe . . .

her maternal grandfather	**de'élel**
fire	**dí'yu**
coyote	**géwe**
wolf	**tulíŕ̌ši'**
Washoe	**waʼšiw**

"It was a bright and sunny morning on *Lake Tahoe*. *Dama'lili*, who was lazy, refused to get up and go hunting with his older brother, *Peweceli*. *Dama'lili* promised to do many chores, clean their camp, and stay out of trouble if *Peweceli* would go without him.

"As soon as *Peweceli* left, *Dama'lili* broke his promises and wandered off. He came upon a **spider's** den and ventured deep inside to watch her weave her web. He asked her many questions, but *Spider* told him to go away because she was busy. He kept right on bothering her and—when she wasn't looking—threw dirt in her web.

"Finally, *Spider* finished her web. 'Would you like to see it?' she asked. *Dama'lili* eagerly replied, 'Yes!' 'Then come closer,' she called. When he got nearer, *Spider* pounced on him and bit him. Very quickly *Dama'lili* died from her poison. Fearing someone would miss him, *Spider* buried *Dama'lili's* body in a hole, then cleaned up to make it look as if nothing had happened.

"*Peweceli* returned to camp to find things still a mess and *Dama'lili* missing. He followed *Dama'lili's* tracks to *Spider's* den and asked if she had seen him. 'No,' she said. 'I've been working on my web all day and have seen no one.' *Peweceli* searched all over but *Dama'lili's* trail always led him back to *Spider's* den. He asked her again if she had seen **his younger brother**. *Spider* became angry and told him to go away.

"*Peweceli* returned to camp and began to cry. Suddenly, a rainbow came down from the sky. A voice that came from all around told him to climb on it. When he did, the rainbow took him to *Sun*. *Sun* told *Peweceli* that he was very displeased that *Spider* had killed *Dama'lili* and then lied about it. *Sun* gave *Peweceli* a pouch of tobacco and told him how to use it. Just before he put *Peweceli* back on the rainbow, *Sun* gave him the power to restore a life just one time.

"As soon as he returned to camp, *Peweceli* went to *Spider's* den. 'Where is *Dama'lili*?' he asked. 'I don't know!' she shouted and ran back down her tunnel. He chased her to her web, then made smoke with the tobacco as *Sun* had instructed him. As the fumes filled the den, *Peweceli* asked *Spider* again where his brother was. 'I don't know,' she said again, coughing hard. *Peweceli* puffed harder on the tobacco. Soon the smoke filled the den and *Spider* died. *Peweceli*, who had been told by *Sun* where to find **his brother**, dug up *Dama'lili* and brought him back to life. The two ran out into the sunshine, happy to

Mele knew that *her grandfather* told this story to remind the **children** always to speak the truth.

The *fire* embers glowed as the **children** were carried to their sleeping *mats*. Soon the entire camp was soothed to sleep by the gentle caresses of the night breezes. The *summer* months passed quickly and happily as the families enjoyed the generous harvests of *fish* and plants from *Lake Tahoe*.

THE LANGUAGE OF THE WASHOE . . .

Lake Tahoe / lake	**dá'aw**	*short-tailed weasel*	**damá'lili'**
long-tailed weasel	**pe'wéčeli'**	*spider*	**čŕkɨ**
his younger brother	**debéyu**	*sun*	**dí·be**
her maternal grandfather	**de'élel**	*fire*	**dí'yu**
mat	**mó·ba'**	*summer*	**čigá·bat**
fish	**'áłabi'**	*children*	**ŋáwŋaŋ**

Mele awoke one morning to the sound of excited voices.

"The *pine nuts* are ready to be picked down in the east valley!" exclaimed the runner. "We must go soon!"

Mele felt both happy and sad. She knew she would miss her friends from the *Northern Washoe*. Time would pass slowly through the long, hard *winter* before they could meet again in the *spring*. Yet Mele was also very excited about the upcoming *pine nut* harvest.

Mele's daydreams of the *pine nut ceremonial gathering* quickly ended as *her mother* gently shook her shoulders and said, "Wake up little one, there are many chores to be done." There was much to do in the next few days to get ready to travel down to the *pine nut* hills.

Mele happily ran over to Hoya's mat. Hoya was already up and had two *water baskets* hanging over her shoulders. Hoya handed one to Mele and the girls scampered through brush and trees. They startled a herd of *deer* on the path down to *Lake Tahoe*. When they reached *the edge of the lake*, Hoya was surprised by the voice of *her father* as he called out, "I'll race you to the floating log." He and Nuki were already in the *lake* for an early morning swim and were paddling along the *lake's* edge.

THE LANGUAGE OF THE WASHOE . . .	
pine nut	**ɫáˑgɨm**
Northern Washoe	**wélmelɫi'**
winter	**gális**
spring	**'ámšak**
ceremonial gathering	**gumsabáy'**
her mother	**dalá'**
water basketry jug	**ḱétep**
deer	**memdéˑwi**
Lake Tahoe / lake	**dá'aw**
the edge of the lake	**dá'aw 'áˑga'a**
her father	**dagóy'**

Hoya dropped her *water basket* on the sand. "Let's go!" she squealed as she jumped in.

Mele only hesitated for a moment and then jumped into the cool water. They swam hard and fast, touching the log at the same time.

"*Father*, I wish we could stay at *Lake Tahoe* forever," Hoya sighed sadly. "*Winter* is so long and cold and *summer* is so much fun here."

"Yes, I know," answered *her father*, "but remember that it gets even colder here in *winter* than down near our *pine nut* lands."

"I love the *pine nut* harvest and the *rabbit drive*. I even like the *winter*," Mele said defensively.

"Mele, you only like *winter* because *your grandfather* tells the best stories," teased Hoya.

Hoya's father then urged them all to swim back to the beach. "Time for play is over and now you must fill the *water baskets*."

So they swam back, filled their *water baskets* and returned to camp.

The Language of The Washoe . . .	
water basketry jug	ǩétep
my father	digóy'
Lake Tahoe / lake	dá'aw
winter	gális
summer	čigáꞏbat
her father	dagóy'
pine nut	ƚáꞏgɩm
rabbit drive	'ušéwe'
your maternal grandfather	'um'élel

The day of their departure dawned clear and rosy. There was even a hint of chill in the air. The members of the *Carson Valley Washoe* and *Northern Washoe* scurried to load up their belongings. The men carried the rolled *mats* with the skins and hides. The women carried their *burden baskets* full of the harvest. Many women carried two *burden baskets* with a strap around their foreheads. Young children were carried in *cradle baskets*. Mele and Toso each had a *burden basket* to carry. There was so much work to be done that everyone had to help.

Mele and Toso sadly hugged Hoya and Nuki goodbye. They promised to meet again next *summer* at *Lake Tahoe*. "Goodbye, goodbye!" shouted the friends as they waved and each family headed down to their *pine nut* hills.

THE LANGUAGE OF THE WASHOE . . .

Carson Valley Washoe	**ṗáʼwaʼluʼ**	*pine nut*	**ťáˑgɨm**
Northern Washoe	**wélmelťiʼ**	*winter*	**gális**
mat	**móˑbaʼ**	*autumn*	**ʼóʼos**
burden basket	**máˑmayʼ**	*her maternal grandfather*	**deʼélel**
cradle basket	**bɨḱus**	*eagle*	**paťálŋiʼ**
summer	**čigáˑbat**	*her mother*	**daláʼ**
Lake Tahoe / lake	**dáʼaw**	*mountain*	**daláʼak**

The families of Mele and Toso had been walking for most of the day when they came to a ledge where they could see the *pine nut* hills and their *winter* valley. The golden colors of *autumn* painted themselves across the horizon. Mele loved this view almost more than the stories of *her grandfather*. She felt as if she could see forever.

"Mele, look at the *eagle* as he soars over us!" exclaimed *her mother*.

"He hunts us for his dinner!" laughed Toso.

"I can outrun the *eagle!*" Mele boasted.

The family laughed and continued the long hike down the *mountain*.

Finally, the *Carson Valley Washoe* arrived in the *pine nut* hills with weary legs and happy hearts. In the evening, after all the families had arrived, the **leader** began the ceremony. Mele and Toso listened intently with their dark eyes sparkling in the firelight as the **leader** welcomed all the families.

"We have been given a very bountiful *pine nut* harvest this year. Let us all celebrate this gift with *food* and dance to show the thankfulness in our hearts. Let the drummers begin our song!"

Mele looked up as **her mother** and *father* joined hands with the other men and women of the tribe. She felt a hand on her shoulder and was happy to know that her best friend, Toso, was near. "I love to watch the happy smiles on the faces of *my mother* and *father* as they dance around the *fire*, don't you, Toso?"

THE LANGUAGE OF THE WASHOE . . .

Carson Valley Washoe	**pá·wa'lu'**
pine nut	**ƚá·gɨm**
leader	**detúmu**
food	**démlu**
her mother	**dalá'**
her father	**dagóy'**
my mother	**dilá'**
my father	**digóy'**
fire	**dí'yu**
women's hockey	**sigá'yak**
ceremonial gathering	**gumsabáy'**

"Oh, yes! But I especially love all the games we will play!" confided Toso. "I hope we will play **hockey**. It's my favorite!"

Mele agreed with her friend, "Yes, there will be games every day, much **food** and dancing every night. The **pine nut ceremonial gathering** is my favorite ceremony of the year."

The days flew by. Mele and Toso gathered with their families for the last night of the ceremonies.

The **leader** stood and led them all in prayer. "We are thankful for the bountiful **pine nuts**. May we share our **food** with others, fill our minds with kind thoughts, and remember to leave some behind. Now let us go down to the **stream** for the cleansing ceremony."

The families solemnly walked down through the **willows** to the water. Mele and Toso listened quietly as the **birds** called out. When they reached the **stream**, they bathed to cleanse their spirits as well as their bodies.

Tomorrow morning would be the first day of the **pine nut** harvest, Mele thought as she went to sleep with a happy smile on her face.

THE LANGUAGE OF THE WASHOE . . .

leader	**detúmu**
pine nut	**ɫáꞏgim**
food	**démlu**
stream	**wáɫa**
willow	**hímu**
bird	**síꞏsu**

The big day arrived. There was a crisp snap in the air, reminding everyone that *winter* was coming. Mele loved to gather *pine cones* that the men and boys knocked down from the trees with their *pine nut gathering poles*. The women and girls gathered the *pine cones* to fill the *burden baskets*. Then the nuts were poured into *tightly woven winnowing baskets* to remove the *pine needles* and dirt. Afterwards, Mele watched *her mother* shake the *pine nuts* in a *winnowing basket* with hot coals to weaken the shells.

A *grinding stone* was then used to break the shells. Some of the nuts were ground into *flour* for a paste used to rub and clean the other nuts.

Toso and Mele ran to the pits the men had dug to store the nuts for *winter*. "*Father*, can we help?" shouted Mele.

"Yes, my child, many hands ease the work," *her father* replied.

They all joined together to fill the pit with *pine nuts*. Once the pit was full, they covered it with a mound of *sagebrush* so they could locate the nuts when they were needed throughout the *winter*. The remaining nuts would be ground into *flour*. It would be made into a *pine nut soup* that would sustain them throughout the cold season.

THE LANGUAGE OF THE WASHOE . . .	
winter	**gális**
pine cone	**yá·ga'**
pine nut gathering pole	**bíhe'**
burden basket	**má·may'**
tightly woven winnowing basket	**mudá·l**
pine needle	**bóyoŋ**
my father	**digóy'**
pine nut	**ɫá·gɨm**
her father	**dagóy'**
wide weave winnowing basket	**ɫugé·bɨl**
grinding stone	**gámum**
flour	**deyétbi'**
sagebrush	**dá·bal**
pine nut soup	**deyú·geli'**

Mele's heart pounded with excitement. Mele's **uncle,** the **jackrabbit** boss, had returned with great news. His strong voice carried over the camp. "My family, a **jackrabbit** gathering lies over to the east of the **pine nuts**. It is time for the **rabbit drive**."

Mele knew that this year she would be allowed to participate.

Frozen dew on the **sagebrush** greeted the family on the morning of the **rabbit drive**. Mele realized that **winter's** snow would soon be upon them. She prayed that today's hunt would be successful with many **jackrabbits** to divide among her people.

THE LANGUAGE OF THE WASHOE . . .

her paternal uncle	**de'éwši'**
jackrabbit	**pélew**
pine nut	** łáˑgɨm**
rabbit drive	**'ušéwe'**
sagebrush	**dáˑbal**
winter	**gális**

"SEA
2001"

"Mele, hurry!" shouted *her mother*. "It is time to go!"

Mele quickly picked up the end of the woven *net*. The family rapidly moved to their end of the line. Slowly the human and *net* barriers surrounded the *jackrabbits*.

Mele's *uncle* had successfully arranged each family and their *net* to form a trap. The *jackrabbits* were driven into the center and would soon be completely surrounded. The *jackrabbits* panicked and raced frantically as they searched for an escape. Mele and Toso's eyes grew wider and wider as the number of captured *jackrabbits* grew to the hundreds.

Suddenly, Toso tripped and yelled out as her legs became tangled in the *net*.

"Toso, get up, get up!" shouted Mele.

"I cannot! My legs are trapped!" Toso cried.

"You must! The *jackrabbits* are coming!" shrieked Mele. She watched in horror as they raced toward them and the flattened *net* that trapped Toso. If the *jackrabbits* escaped, Mele and Toso would be shamed and their families could go hungry this *winter*.

"Toso, Toso, you must get up!" Mele yelled into the swirling dust and confusion.

Then, Mele saw *her uncle* scoop Toso up under his arm. He carried her along with the *net* in which she was still entangled. The *net* was once again stretched into a barrier. She saw *her uncle* quickly free Toso's legs and set her down,

so she could once again walk and help hold the *net*. Mele was so grateful for his wisdom and strength.

"Now!" shouted *her uncle*.

Mele and the others threw the *net* down to trap the animals. Then her people started the hard work of slaughtering the animals. Mele's arms began to burn from swinging the club.

After many hours, Mele fell to the ground numb with exhaustion as she watched *her mother*, *father* and *uncle* still hard at work.

THE LANGUAGE OF THE WASHOE . . .

her mother	**dalá'**
net	**dírges**
jackrabbit	**pélew**
her paternal uncle	**de'éwši'**
winter	**gális**
her father	**dagóy'**

The next few weeks were busy for the family. Their days were filled with work to prepare them for the cold days ahead. They divided up the *jackrabbit skins* equally among all the families. Now the women were busy smoking the meat to prepare it for *winter*. Others were sewing the furs into *jackrabbit blankets* to be used during the short days and long cold nights of *winter*.

Mele was tired of all the work, but she knew it had to be done before the *falling snow* came.

THE LANGUAGE OF THE WASHOE . . .

jackrabbit skins	**pélew 'íš**
winter	**gális**
jackrabbit blankets	**pélew 'ís dípi'**
falling snow	**dedé'es**

Sleep came easily to Mele and she was soon breathing the gentle rhythm of a dreaming child. She awoke suddenly from her deep sleep. The silence of the early morning hours had crept into her dreams of swimming at *Lake Tahoe*. She snuggled deeper into her *jackrabbit blankets* when she realized that the tingles on her cheeks were from the snow drifting into their *winter house*.

"*Mother, Mother!*" she whispered urgently. "The snow has come. *Winter* is here!"

"Yes, Mele, my dear, *winter* is here," *her mother* whispered back. "*Winter* follows *autumn, autumn* follows *summer, summer* follows *spring*, and *spring* follows *winter*. These are seasons of our lives, our *Washoe* life."

Mele smiled as she drifted back to sleep surrounded by her loving family.

THE LANGUAGE OF THE WASHOE . . .

Lake Tahoe	**dá'aw**
jackrabbit blankets	**pélew 'íɾs dípi'**
winter house	**gális dáŋal**
my mother	**dilá'**
winter	**gális**
her mother	**dalá'**
autumn	**'ó'os**
summer	**čigaɾ́bat**
spring	**'ámšak**
Washoe	**waɾ́šiw**

Glossary

ʾámšak – spring
ʾáƚabi' – fish
bíhe' – pine nut gathering pole
biƙus – cradle basket
bóšdi' – wild onion
bóyoŋ – pine needle
čigáˑbat – summer
číˑkɨ – spider
dáʾaw – lake / Lake Tahoe
dáʾaw ʾáˑgaʾa – on the shore / edge of the lake
dáˑbal – sagebrush
dagóy' – his / her / their father
dalá' – his / her / their mother
dalá'ak – mountain
damáˑlili' – short-tailed weasel
debéyu – (his / her / their) younger brother
dedé'eš – falling snow
de'élel – his / her / their maternal grandfather
de'éwši' – his / her / their paternal uncle
démge' – stone grinding surface
démlu – food
detúmu – leader, boss
deyétbi' – flour
deyúˑgeli' – pine nut soup
díˑbe – sun or moon
díˑgeš – net
digóy' – my / our father
dilá' – my / our mother
dípi' – blanket
dí'yu – fire
gális – winter
gális dáŋal – winter house
gámum – grinding stone
géwe – coyote
gumsabáy' – ceremonial gathering
háŋaleƚi' – Southern Washoe
hímu – willow
ƙétep – basketry water jug
ƙómol – ball

maʾálaŋi' – wild strawberry
máˑmay' – burden basket
memdéˑwi – deer
móˑba' – mat
mudáˑl – tightly woven winnowing basket
ŋáwŋaŋ – baby, child
ʾóʾos – autumn
paƚálŋi' – eagle
ṗáˑwaʾlu' – Carson Valley Washoe
pélew – jackrabbit
pélew ʾíˑš – rabbit skin
pélew ʾíˑs dípi' – rabbit skin blanket
pe'wéčeli' – long-tailed weasel
sigá'yak – women's hockey
síˑsu – bird
ƚáˑgɨm – pine nut
ƚáˑƚat – magpie
ƚétɨk – seed
ƚugéˑbɨl – wide weave winnowing basket
tulíˑši' – wolf
ʾum'élel – your maternal grandfather
ʾušéwe' – rabbit drive
wáˑšiw – Washoe
wáƚa – stream, river
wélmelƚi' – Northern Washoe
yáˑga' – pine cone

WASHOE PRONUNCIATION

As Washoe has some sounds not found in English, some special symbols are required to accurately indicate pronunciation. (Washoe has a few additional sounds not listed here, which do not occur in the words used in this story.)

- The following symbols indicate sounds similar to those in English:

  b d ġ h k l m p s t w y

- š sounds like *sh* in *ship* or *dish*
- ŋ sounds like *ng* in *sing* or *long*
- ' (apostrophe) indicates a "glottal stop," a quick catch in the throat. It occurs in English, for example, in *uh-oh* (as though you're in trouble), at the beginning of each syllable.
- The ' above consonants (č k̓ p̓ ṱ) indicates their "glottalized" counterpart. A glottal stop is produced simultaneously with the consonant. The closure in the throat must be maintained until after the closure in the mouth is released. č sounds like *ts* in *hats*, but with a glottalized ṱ.
- An accent mark over a vowel (such as á í ú) indicates the stressed symbol of a word.
- The · after a vowel (such as á· í· ú·) indicates a long vowel, with a duration longer than that of a short vowel (such vowels are also stressed).
- The six vowel letters used have "continental" values. The following rough comparisons of long vowel qualities to those in English can be made:

  á· sounds like *a* in *father*

  é· varies between *e* as in *pet* and *pep* or *a* as in *bad* and *ash*

  í· sounds like *ee* in *see* or *keep*

  ɨ· sounds somewhat like *u* in *just* (as in he's *just* come in). This vowel symbol may be referred to as "barred-i."

  ó· sounds like *au* in *caught* for English dialects where this is different from *cot*, or *o* in *wore*.

  ú· sounds like *oo* in *soon* and *hoop*

- The short vowels (whether stressed or not) show the following approximate English ones:

  a varies between *a* as in *father* and *u* as in *hut* or *put*

  e sounds like *e* as in *pet* or *pep*

  i sounds like *i* in *hip* or *pit*

  ɨ sounds somewhat like *u* in *just*

  o sounds like *o* in *go*, but shorter

  u sounds like *u* in *putt* and *oo* in *book*

- Note also the following dipthongs:

  ay sounds like *i* in *ice* or *fine*

  aw sounds like *ou* in *house* and *ow* in *cow*

Pronunciation guide courtesy of Professor William H. Jacobsen, Jr.

Recommended Reading

For Children:

Brother Eagle, Sister Sky, Chief Seattle, Jeffers, Susan (Illus.), New York: Dial Books for Young Readers, 1991.

Buffalo Hunt, Freedman, Russell, New York: Holiday House, 1995.

Dance on a Sealskin, Winslow, Barbara, Sloat, Teri (Illus.) Anchorage: Alaska Northwest Books, 2002.

Knots on a Counting Rope, Archambault, John, Martin, Jr., Bill (Illus), New York: Owlet, 1997.

The Last American Rainforest TONGASS, Gill, Shelley, and Shannon Cartwright (Illus.), Paws IV, Publications, 1997.

The Legend of Mackinac Island, Wargin, Kathy-jo,. Van Frankenhuyzen, Gijsbert (Illus.), Chelsea, MI: Sleeping Bear Press, 1999.

A River Ran Wild: An Environmental History, Cherry, Lynne, San Diego: Voyager Books, 2002.

Thirteen Moons on a Turtle's Back: A Native Year of Moons, Burchac, Joseph, and London, Jonathan, New York: Scholastic, 1992.

For Adults and Teachers

Beginning Washo, Jacobsen, William H., Jr., Nevada State Museum, Occasional Papers 5. Pp. iv +58, 1996.

Ethnographic Notes on the Washo, Lowie, Robert H., University of California Publications in American Archaeology and Ethnology 36.301-352, 1939.

Handbook of North American Indians, Volume 11: Great Basin, d'Azevedo, Warren L., Washoe. Pp. 466-498 in Warren L.d'Azevedo, ed., *See also* Fowler, Catherine S., and Dawson, Lawrence E., pp.705-708, 729-731, 735-736 Washington: Smithsonian Institution, 1986.

The Two Worlds of the Washo, An Indian Tribe of California and Nevada, Downs, James F., New York: Holt, Rinehart and Winston. Pp. xii + 113., 1966.

Wa She Shu: A Washo Tribal History, Nevers, Jo Ann, Reno: Inter-Tribal Council of Nevada, 1976.

The Washo Indians: History, Life cycle, Religion, Technology, Economy and Modern Life, Price, John A., Nevada State Museum Occasional Papers 4, 1980.

Washo Tales, Translated with an Introduction, Dangberg, Grace, Nevada State Museum Occasional Papers 1. Pp. [v] + 103, 1968 .